3 A STORMGATE PRESS

ZANE CARRINGTON

CHARLES F. MILLHOUSE

stormgatepress.com
stormgatepress@gmail.com

First Printing: 2024
ISBN: 9798325754425
Imprint: Independently published

Introducing the Stormgate Press Quick Read Books

Short Story Pulp Adventure Books
reminiscent of the dime store novels of old.

BOOK 1: The Purple Mystique

BOOK 2: Night Vision

BOOK 3: A Zane Carrington Adventure

Watch for more books in the series coming soon...

THE SECRET PROMISE OF HARRY TUCKER

A man's life is important to him, unless he's playing for money. Money has the power to manipulate those who have it, those who want it, and those who seek it. When money is involved, people tend to forget what's important to them, including their life.

I see it all the time. Shanghai harbor is a magnet for the deprived and those seeking fortune any way they can. Game nights at Shin Wan Harry's, brought out the most atrocious of individuals. It's a festering place for those willing to gamble away all they have for a chance to win big.

It was a Saturday night in the spring of 1936 when the weekly card night turned into something much more. As I look back on it now, there was no way of knowing the secrets I would learn, secrets that would test the foundation of friendship.

My name is Zane Carrington, I'm the captain of the Algiers, a tramp steamer that hauls cargo to ports all over Southeast Asia. I won't bore you with the details as to how I became captain because it's not important to this event. Being a wanted man in the United States has a way of making a person keep a low profile, but that's a lesson I've been unable to learn.

Shin Wan Harry's was a dive at the end of the pier. In most respects the place should have been condemned. The walls were tinted yellow with nicotine, the floors were sticky with years of spilled beer, dripped blood and sweat from years of barfights, and gunplay. Many of them I'm ashamed to say, I was involved in. Still, despite its reputation, the establishment was packed most nights and, on the weekends, the rented rooms above the bar were filled with wayward souls either needing to rent them for the night or by the hour. As long as money came in his direction, Harry didn't care.

Harry Tucker was an Australian with dark raven hair, though to tell the truth I didn't know much about him. He was a burly man, with large, weathered hands, and a handsome face with deep age line crisscrossing and marring his features. He definitely had seen his fair share of hard life. The stories I heard about him matched his windswept appearance, but like most folk in this part of the world, he didn't talk about his past and I didn't want to know. If Harry wanted to tell me, he would have. I felt it was better that way.

The weather in this part of the world was sticky and hot, and hot was putting it mildly. On most days your clothes would be wet and stuck to you as if you had taken a bath in them. Fill the saloon with twenty people or more, and the rackety old ceiling fan above you might as well not even be on.

The players in the Saturday card game varied from week to week, depending on who happened to be in port. Whenever I was in town, I would sit in. Hell, there wasn't much to do besides get drunk or pay for a prostitute and if I couldn't get a woman for free, there wasn't much need in having one.

Besides me, there were five others at the table. Harry, of course and the sniveling rat Cyrus Gray who never missed a game. The others in the group, I had never met before. They probably came in on the Pan Am Clipper, or by other means. Everyone had a story, and like Harry, not many were forthcoming. The three newcomers to the game were ready to play. All of them dubious and all of them, reserved.

I always fancied myself as some wild west gambler like the kind found in a Howard Donovan western novel, but unlike those smooth characters portrayed in a book, I had the tendency to lose the shirt off my back if I wasn't careful. I am pretty good at reading people, but not always when it comes to cards.

The woman at the table, a lovely red head with sharp mesmerizing eyes and smooth milky skin hadn't been in the Asian sun long. She wore a dark conservative dress that buttoned at her neck – the heat didn't seem to bother her much. She wore no jewelry but did have a silver brooch pinning back her scarlet locks. She didn't say much, only that her name was Naples, she didn't give a last name, but few ever did.

Harry delt the first hand. The game was five card stud with nothing wild. Naples kept each card turned down to the table as they were placed in front of her.

"Aren't you going to look at your cards, my dear?" an Arab, that sat next to Naples asked with a lilt of a laugh in his words, as if he saw the woman as an easy mark.

"I'll mind my own cards, and ask that you regard your own hand, sir," Naples said in her heavy Australian accent not making eye contact with the man.

The Arab was lanky, and balding. He wore an old thread worn suit that needed some serious laundering, that matched his dark rimmed spectacles with the right lens chipped slightly in the corner.

"The lady is right," the third newcomer said with a Texan drawl in his tone. This made me be wary of him for a couple of reasons. One, he was American, plus in the few instances that a bounty hunter had come looking for me, some of them had been from Texas. I'm not sure why, mind you, maybe it's because Texans fancied themselves gunslingers, or loyal Americans, or they simply liked to get paid for bringing someone in to collect some coin. Either way, I meant to keep a watchful eye on the Texan.

"I don't need you to come to my rescue," Naples said with a sharp glare at the Texan.

"Excuse me," the Texan said tipping back his oversize cowboy hat.

"By your vocabulary I say you were from Kulgera," Harry said in a friendly gesture.

"Alice Springs, if it's all the same to you," Naples said.

"Ah, an inlander," Harry said with a smile.

Naples only reply was an annoyed look and Harry rolled his lower lip and hitched a laugh, as if he had been put in his place.

4

"I take it, you're not much for conversation," I said directing my question to Naples. She didn't look up from her cards. "I've never known Australians to be so quiet."

"Some of us aren't as forthcoming, Mr. Carrington. We only say what's important."

"You know my name?" I asked with a raised eyebrow.

Naples rolled her eyes up to look at me, and said, "I heard talk of a tramp steamer captain by the name of Carrington who liked to hear himself talk and I assumed it was you."

Harry rolled with laughter, slapping the palms of his hands on the table in front of him, spilling some of the drinks. "Oy, she put you in your place, Zane," he said trying to control his laughter.

I stared at the pretty young woman and smiled when she offered one of her own. Taking a cigar from the inside of my shirt pocket I struck a match and lit the stogie, while I tried to sum her up. On one hand she was callous. She went to great lengths to paint herself as uncommunicative, and standoffish. Yet there was something else about her. Everyone came to this part of the world for a reason, and though I didn't know why she came to Shanghai she went to great strives to keep that to herself. *But why go out of her way to call me by name?* I wondered. She didn't have to say my name. In fact, she didn't have to recognize me at all. There was something more to it, she wanted me to know she knew my name. *Why?*

The night wore on, having lost more games than I won, I bowed out for the remainder of the hands. Around midnight, I sat at the bar sipping a beer and nibbling on old peanuts that tasted more like rust and soggy beans, than what they should have tasted like. Jib, the bartender was of little conversation that night. He was busy talking up one of the local call girls, Hoshi, maybe looking for a little company after he was finished at work. Either way, I wasn't alone long.

When Naples approached, she ordered herself a cold one, and she was quickly served, Jib didn't have time to sling beer when he was close to coming to terms with Hoshi.

Naples sat two stools away from me, and I asked her, "You give up for the night?"

"The wind was turning, I didn't see any reason to continue," she said, not looking away from her glass.

"Considering you took most of my money, I figure you did alright," I said.

"Perhaps I was having more of a good time watching you lose," Naples replied.

Her quick wit led me to believe she was more intelligent than most of the people that ended up here at Harry's. If she was simply passing through Shanghai, then why come here? There were more respectable places in the city than some dive on the docks.

Swallowing down the last bit of my beer, I almost choked on it when Naples asked, "Do you want to get out of here?"

I'm sure my expression was one of confusion and shock. If anything, the last thing I would have expected was being propositioned by her. I would have thought Jib would have worked out a deal quicker than Naples offering to leave with me.

Not one to turn down female companionship, especially one as lovely as Naples, it didn't take me long to acquiesce and in less than a minute later she and I were headed toward the door of the bar. I turned back to Harry who appeared to be engaged in heavy conversation with the Texan and the Arab. Cyrus Gray had bowed out along while ago, and Harry glanced in my direction, and I offered him a nod, but he did not acknowledge my departure, which at the time I didn't find peculiar.

Outside, the sultry heat wore heavy on the lungs. The common sounds of the marina filled the night, and there were still quite a few people out, considering Shanghai was a major port, I'd be surprised if it wasn't busy.

Surprisingly, Naples seemed more approachable than she did earlier in the evening. She took my arm, laughed at my jokes, and seemed very inviting. Remember when I said I had a knack for reading people? This was one of those occasions. It didn't take me long to realize she was putting on an act.

We weren't even out of sight of the saloon when I stopped, turned toward her and said, "What's the deal?"

"I don't understand," Naples replied innocently.

Now, I'm no fool, though there would be a few people... well okay, a lot of people who would think I am, but I've been around long enough to know when I was being taken for a ride. Naples used my gender in her favor, batting her eyes, and offering me a night with a pretty woman and all to her favor and I fell for it hook, line and sucker. "I want to know why you wanted me out of the bar."

Again, Naples gave me a strange, confused look. Back in the game she knew me by reputation, not surprised by my name. In which case she knew what kind of man I was, especially when it came to my friends. She wanted me out of the bar for a reason. And then it dawned on me. That look. The one Harry gave me when I was leaving. Almost saying, without saying, I'm in trouble.

I grabbed Naples by the arms, gripping her tight in my hands. Pulling her toward me I asked, "What gives? Why did you want me out of Harry's?"

"You're hurting me," she said. Perhaps I was, but her naïveté only went so far.

"Don't play games with me."

She struggled against my pull, and I realized I wasn't going to get anything out of her. Pushing her away I headed back for the saloon. I heard her call my name, but by that time I stopped listening, she wasn't answering any of my questions anyway.

When I entered the saloon I heard Jib call, "for Pete's sake Zane, get down!" I saw Harry being manhandled by the Arab, and there were several other men, who weren't involved in the game, but were helping him.

I dove for cover behind the bar with Jib when the Texan opened fire with a very large and a very noisy gun. Chunks of the bar top splintered down on us as I stared into Jibs dark eyes. "What the hell is happening?"

8

"I wish I could say," Jib said. "A minute or two after you went out, all hell broke loose."

Although Jib was just as much in the dark as I was, I did have a bit more insight into what was happening than he did. Naples was definitely involved, to what capacity, I wasn't sure. Her being Australian should have been a dead giveaway, but with this part of the world a melting pot for all types of cultures, it wasn't always wise to categorize people by their ethnicity. This time however I would have been right... yay me.

"Shotgun?" I asked Jib. "Where is the shotgun?"

"You're not armed?" the aging Asian asked.

"Contrary to popular belief most Americans don't walk around with a gun strapped to their hip," I replied. "It's not like in the cowboy pictures."

Jib's brow furrowed and he just stared at me in disbelief. I rarely left the *Algiers* with my gun. Even in Shanghai gun-toting individuals were scrutinized by the local police. "Just give me the shotgun."

"It won't do you any good," Jib said. "There haven't been any bullets in it for six months."

Only a fool would go into a gun fight with an empty gun, I told myself. "Give me the gun," I said with confidence. Without a complaint, Jib pulled the shotgun from under the bar and handed it to me.

"Stay put," I said.

"You don't have to tell me twice," he replied.

I went out from behind the bar, gun in hand, confidence etched on my face as I cocked the gun – it made a scary click-clack sound and I pointed it toward the Texan and

9

said with weight to my words, "Let Harry go, or I'll blow your head clear off."

"Uh, Zane," Harry said with a tone as to tell me the gun wasn't loaded. I ignored him.

"I can't miss at this range," I told the Texan.

"If'n you were going to pull the trigger, I suspect you would have done it by now," the Texan said.

He was right. If the shotgun would have been loaded, I would have already killed him. Instead, I went a different route and said, "Well maybe I just didn't want to mess the place up with your blood."

"Would you be able to tell?" the Texan asked.

"Hey..." Harry protested.

"Not now Harry, the grownups are talking," I said keeping my eyes pinned on the oversized cowboy. "What's it going to be Tex? We going to stand here all day, have a shootout, or call it a tie and you get the hell out of here."

"Uh Zane..."

"I said not now Harry."

When a flash of light exploded behind my eyes, I lost control of all bodily functions, and before I realized it, the floor jumped up and smacked me in the face.

I woke with Jib over me and a band of mariachis playing an annoying tune inside my head. Stars twirled in my vision, and although Jib was saying something, I had no idea what it was. He lay a cold hand on my face, and in time I was able to understand what he was saying. "Zane, Zane, can you hear me."

"Not so loud," I said. "You're drowning out the music."

"What?" Jib asked with a confused tone.

"Never mind," I said. "Help me up."

On my feet, the world swirled. Shaking off the feeling was difficult, and with a little help, I sat on a stool at the bar. Studying the saloon, there wasn't a living soul in it, except me and Jib. "What the hell happened? I was certain the Texan was going to walk away."

"I thought so too," Jib said. "Until the woman hit you from behind."

"Woman... what woman?"

"The one you went out with," Jib said passing me a glass of water.

Taking a swig, and curling my nose, I said, "Beer, give me a beer." Studying Jib as he crossed to the other side of the bar, I asked. "How long have I been out?"

"Forty minutes," Jib replied. "I sent someone to your ship to tell them what happened, but no one has showed up yet."

I hitched a laugh. My crew often jested that if there was trouble around, I'd be in the middle of it. You know, sometimes I don't think my crew cares much for the adventures I get into. I shook off that thought, regarded Jib, and asked, "They took Harry, didn't they?"

"Aye," Jib said. "Not long after you hit the floor."

Thinking straight wasn't an option. A London fog hung around me and even if I wanted too, I couldn't rush out looking for Harry. I needed to find out who Naples was, what relationship she had with Harry and maybe then, I could start piecing together where they took him.

About that time Ronald P. Chesterton III came through the door. Ronald was a Major, retired of His Majesties army, and for the last couple of years he had been living on the *Algiers*. Ronald was in his late sixties with a round midsection and a full white beard with hair to match. He was always impeccably dressed wearing only the finest of clothes from Ede and Ravenscroft and specially couriered to him from London, since he had fallen out of favor with the government and could not return, for reasons that allude me.

"What have you gotten yourself into this time?" Ronald asked, wiping off a spot on the bar with a handkerchief before leaning against it.

Ronald might be a number of things. A bit snooty, standoffish and a little misogynistic, but he was a good confidant. A brilliant tactician who on many occasions saved my ass and it didn't take me long to explain to him what happened, or at least my version of events.

With the sound of annoyance in his tone, Ronald asked, "And I take it, you want to find Harry?"

"I know you don't come here a lot, Major, but this place is just as much my home as the *Algiers*, and these people are friends of mine," I said regarding, Jib. By the expression on the old Asian's face, he was more concerned about Harry than I was. They were more than working partners, they were friends and the old guy seemed beside himself with worry.

Not commenting on my relationship to the people in the saloon, the Major got right down to the point. "Then I suggest you go to the Australian consulate and find out what you can about this woman."

"You really think she would go there, especially if she was here to cause trouble?" I asked.

"Maybe," The Major replied. "Otherwise, you might find something out about her. And if she came in on the Pan Am Clipper, its most likely she was met by a customs officer upon arrival. I mean, unless you have another idea, that's a good place to start."

Without argument, Ronald was right, but it wasn't until I asked, "You'll go there with me?" that the Major replied adamantly, "No, my boy. This one you will have to do on your own."

I didn't question his reasonings for not going with me. Once the Major made-up his mind there was little changing it. Assuring Jib I would do my best in finding Harry, I left him to clean up the saloon so the bar could open the next day and prepare for business. Jib stated, "If Harry knew I didn't open the bar over a little thing like his kidnapping, he would be furious that he lost business, and you know what Harry always says about business."

"No business, no money, no money... no money," I snorted as I left the bar and headed to the *Algiers*. A shower and change of clothes might help clear this fog that settled over me after I was coldcocked. If you've never been knocked out before, just take it from a guy that has had it happen on several occasions, it's something that stays with you. There's no shaking it off. It just needs to fade away on its own."

The *Algiers*, built in 1924 by Wintergreen Shipping was from stem to stern, three-hundred and ninety feet long. There were bits of rust here and there, and it wasn't the cleanest maritime vessel on the ocean, but she was mine, and no one could take her from me.

She was a big ship to be crewed by only four of us. Soon after taking command, and managing to purchase the ship from Orman Wintergreen, those who were supportive of Captain Halgraves, the previous master of the ship, refused to work for me, leaving only a drunk engineer, a teenage stowaway, and a deposed British military commander as my crew. Where it would have been nice to have a full complement, I was left with Major Chesterton, Lucas with no last name and Crocker, who were like family to me, and we faced life and death together.

I met Lucas on the deck after I cleaned up. Lucas was a wiry kid with unruly dark hair, and buck teeth. Sometimes I felt as if I should know him, his features were familiar to me, but after all the people I have met over the years, faces began to look the same. Still, he was a hard worker and despite our age differences, good friends.

"The Major said I could go with you," Lucas said with enthusiasm.

"He did, did he?" I asked scouring the deck, looking for Ronald. Leave it to the Major to volunteer others when he was unwilling to help. "Look, kid. This might be dangerous..."

Lucas laughed. "When is it never dangerous?" he asked.

The kid had a point. Seems my life was one dangerous episode after another. In the time Lucas had been sailing with me, we both had fallen under gunfire, met crazed enemies and even faced some supernatural beings, which I always try to avoid. "Alright, Lucas," I said. "You can come, but you have to do what I say."

"When don't I ever listen to you?" Lucas asked.

"That's a conversation for another time," I replied. "I don't know what we are walking into, it could be anything and I just want you to know that before we go."

"Zane, I've come to expect things like this on a daily basis," Lucas said. "Look we haven't had a cargo run in the last seven days, if I stay on this ship another day to listen to Crocker singing drunken sea shanties, or Ronald reading Shakespeare out loud I think I'll go insane."

"Come on," I said. "But tuck in your shirt and try and act respectable. We are headed to the Australian consulate, and I would like to put on a good face. Sometimes you have to sweet talk people to get them to listen to you."

"I can't wait to witness your diplomatic skills firsthand," Lucas said with a lilt of a laugh in his words.

The Australian consulate wasn't a very big building, it was surrounded by a tall iron fence but was well manicured and seemed somewhat out of place in the middle of Shanghai. At the front gate stood two uniformed soldiers who stopped us as we approached. "Oy, what business do you have here?" one of the officers asked.

"We are here inquiring about one of your citizens," I told him, and adding a little lie to my statement, I said, "She's missing, and we are concerned about her wellbeing."

I didn't know if they believed my story, but one of the guards went to a phone and called into the main building. "State your name," the guard asked from the small hutch.

"Zane Carrington," I replied, fully aware that once I stepped into the consulate, I would be on Australian soil and could be extradited back to the United States for my crime. I would have to take that risk if I was going to find Harry.

After a long minute, the guard hung up the phone, motioned toward me, and when Lucas and I approached the gate, he said jabbing a finger at me, "Just you. He'll have to wait out here."

I glanced back at Lucas. "Hang here, this probably won't take too long."

"You sure about that?" Lucas asked.

I cocked my mouth to one side, thought about that a second, but didn't offer a reply as I followed the guard through the gate, and up a long sidewalk toward the front of the consulate. Even though I was in Shanghai, when I entered the building, it felt as if I was whisked away to another place. In most locations throughout the city the Asian lifestyle was very much present wherever you went. In the consulate however, it reminded me of a ranch house that I stayed in when I was a kid on vacation with my parents. It felt very much like home.

I was greeted by a man in a three-piece suit with wire thin glasses and a dark flowing beard. He offered a smile when I approached and reached out his hand. When we clasped hands he said, "I'm Ambassador Rodrick Hanover, how might I help you?"

"Ambassador?" I replied taken aback. "I thought I'd see a secretary, or adjutant, but I didn't think I would meet the ambassador."

He gave a toothy smile, and said with confidence, "This is a small posting. To tell you the truth no one else wanted the job, that's why I'm here. The only staff you see is standing right in front of you."

I drew a cleansing breath. With such a small outpost, it was unlikely Hanover knew me by name, or by reputation. I know, I know what you're thinking. Even though my crime is unforgivable in most parts of the civilized world, Zane Carrington was a small fish in a very big fishbowl. The chances of him knowing my name was highly unlikely, but without a full staff to keep him apprised of such things I didn't feel as though I was going to be arrested and taken back to New York in irons.

Hanover led me to his office, a cozy nook filled with stacks of books, reams of paper and large filing cabinets. There were very few personal items besides a photograph of him in a rugby uniform standing alongside a dozen or more men his age. He offered me a drink, which I accepted, and he poured a glass of Scotch.

"I understand you're looking for someone," he said when he gestured to a chair and then sat down behind his messy desk.

"A woman named Naples," I said. "She's Australian, five-two with red hair."

"And your relationship to her?" Hanover asked.

"She's an acquaintance," I said.

"Quite an undertaking to be concerned for an acquaintance," Hanover said.

"She made an impression," I said, still feeling the knot she put on the back of my head. "You know, Shanghai is not a very hospitable place for a woman alone. I'm concerned something might have happened to her, and I simply wanted to check to make sure she is okay."

"But you have no address, no means of finding her, so you came here?"

I grimaced; I was never good at lying off the cuff. Thinking fast I said, "We met at a local saloon, we had a few drinks, some laughs, when I went to the loo, and came back she was gone. It's that simple."

"And you don't think she wasn't interested in you, and left?"

I shrugged, and said, "If you would have seen how she was reacting to me, you wouldn't believe that. Look−" I said flatly. "If you're not going to help me..."

Hanover raised a hand and said, "It's my job to ask questions. I need to know that a citizen is not in any danger before I help you track her down. You don't know her last name, or what brought her to Shanghai, so I have to be cautious."

"I assumed she came in on the clipper, and I hoped you would have a record of her arrival. If you do, you could send someone to where she is staying and..."

"I'm afraid no one fitting her description came in on the clipper," Hanover said.

My shoulders slumped. Finding Naples and Harry was proving more difficult than I thought it would be. Before I could find a way to wriggle out of the office, Hanover added, "There was a private yacht that arrived in Shanghai two days ago. With ships coming and going on the regular, it's difficult to check every vessel coming into port."

I perked up. "What's the name of the yacht?" I asked.

"Since it left the harbor about an hour ago, I guess it wouldn't hurt to tell you. It's called the *RS Eden.*" He said flipping through some papers, until he pulled a sheet out from the stack and added, "Bound for Sydney with a crew of ten, and four passengers. A woman and three men."

"That must be her," I said, placing my glass on the table and standing up hoping to make a quick exit. "Seems she wasn't as attracted to me as I hoped." I offered a fake smile. "That ends that. The woman of my dreams slipped through my fingers... again," I joked. "I guess I'll be going."

Hanover stood from his desk. "What aren't you telling me, Mr. Carrington?"

My mouth bled dry. "What do you mean?" I asked.

"I might not be the sharpest tack in the box, but I do know when someone is giving me a cock and bull story. There's more to it, isn't there?"

Trying to be as honest as I could, I said, "She took something that's important to me. I want it back."

"And you didn't think going to the police should have been your first stop?"

"The Shanghai police aren't very helpful when it comes to someone from the west," I said. "I could have gone there

19

but I still would have ended up here. Either way, it doesn't matter, she's gone, and I need to go."

Hanover came around his desk and before I could turn, he snagged me by the arm. His grip was tight, and I regarded the rugby photograph and then set my sights on him. This man was strong, and it wouldn't do me any good to try and fight my way out.

"Look," I said. "She's out of your jurisdiction, especially now that she has left the harbor. She has what she took from me, and I mean to get it back. Are you going to stop me?"

For the next several seconds I wasn't sure what Hanover was going to do. We stared intently at one another for what seemed like forever until finally he released his grip and said, "I'll probably never know the whole story about this, will I, Mr. Carrington?"

"No, I don't think you will," I replied.

"You know, that might be the first truthful thing you said to me since we first shook hands," Hanover replied and then with a stern warning he said, "I think it best that the next time you come to me for help, you have a more convincing story, Mr. Carrington."

I don't know how he knew I was lying to him, maybe because even though my story was laced with half-truths, I didn't totally believe it myself. "Yeah," I said, "I think you're right."

The *Algiers* steamed out of the harbor an hour later. The *RS Eden* had a good two-hour start on us, but a private yacht usually could only make ten knots, where the *Algiers* could easily make twelve, or more if the waters were calm. Thick black smoke poured out of the single stack, and I told Crocker, "Push the engines to their fullest, we have to catch that ship before nightfall, otherwise we don't have a chance in hell of doing so."

Always one to keep me on an even keel, Ronald pointed out, "You sure you know what you're doing, lad? We don't know the reasoning behind Harry's abduction. They could be bounty hunters bringing him to justice for a past crime."

He made a point. As a wanted man myself I know what it's like to watch your back. "All the more reason for me to catch them," I said.

"Zane, you can't be the protector of every wanted man, we don't know what crime Harry could have committed."

"Assuming he is guilty of a crime," I pointed out. "That's why we are in pursuit, to find out."

"It wouldn't do me any good to say, this isn't any of our business, would it?"

I shot Ronald a stern look, by his expression it was a harsher look than I intended. Still by my insipid glare he cleared his throat, fiddled with his shirt collar, and said, "No, I guess it wouldn't."

The thought of condemning an innocent man didn't sit well with me. There might have been a number of reasons Naples wanted Harry, but she didn't strike me as the bounty hunter type.

Two hours later I stood alone in the wheelhouse. Ahead of us a black speck sat on the horizon, and even with binoculars I couldn't make out what kind of vessel it was, but I would bet money it was the ship we were after. I used the E.O.T to signal the engine room. E.T.O stood for engine order telegraph and was used to communicate with Crocker in the engine room. Slipping the guide arms into place, I called for more speed from the engines and several seconds later more black smoke chugged from the stack. At our present speed I thought we would catch the *Eden* before night for sure, but that was wishful thinking.

When Lucas burst into the wheelhouse in a terrified state, he said, "Zane you have to go down to the deck, you have to go down, now."

The thought of telling him to calm down never entered my mind. By the horror in his eyes something was wrong. I drew a breath to ask him, when the Texan came through the door a second later with his very large gun pointed out in front of him.

"What in the name of God, is going on here?" I demanded.

The cowboy gave a toothy smile and said, "You seem like a smart guy, you figure it out. Stop the ship."

With furrowed brow I gave the Texan a sour expression. "You want me to stop the ship?" I asked.

He pulled back the hammer on his gun, took the Lord's name in vain and said with a growl, "Stop the ship, now...!"

I signaled the engine room full stop, and within a minute the *Algiers* slowed in the water. I glared at the cowboy. "Out," he demanded with a wave of his gun and Lucas, and I did as he ordered.

Down onto the deck below the wheelhouse, I found Ronald and Crocker being held at gunpoint by the Arab and another large man that I figured was a crewman from the

Eden. Slumped at Ronald's feet sat Harry Tucker. His face was swollen and looked like clumps of red clay had been molded to his face, if I didn't know it was Harry by his clothes, I would be hard pressed to know it was him.

I regarded Harry. "How," I asked.

"It was very simple to sneak onto your ship, Captain Carrington," Naples said when she approached from behind.

Wheeling around toward her, I found Naples dressed in all black, right down to her laced up, leather boots. Her red hair was pulled into a ponytail at the back of her head, and she wore no makeup, yet there was a plain beauty to her.

Forgetting I was still at gunpoint, I took a step toward her. I ignored the Texan when he said, "Easy there now." There were three things I didn't like: When someone lied to me, when someone cheated me and when someone thought what was mine, was there's. The *Algiers* was my ship and I'd be damned if someone was going to pirate it, especially when I was still alive and able to fight back.

"You have a lot of nerve," I told Naples.

"It's not my fault you are stupid Mr. Carrington," Naples replied. "To tell you the truth the stories about you seem a little farfetched. I heard you were a man that shouldn't be philandered. You see, I needed you out of the way. By your reputation you are a man loyal to your friends and If I took Harry, you would be hard pressed to find him. I knew you wouldn't give up, so I gave you a ship to chase while hiding in your hold. Your man on guard was drunk and passed out, so it was simple to get aboard your ship without being seen."

I shot Crocker a irritable glance. I knew when I hired him, he was a drunk, and unable to keep a job. He had been fired from every ocean liner company in business and he just needed a break. I couldn't be mad at him. He was an alcoholic. If anything, it was my fault for having him on guard. He stared at the deck but rolled his eyes up to me like a sorry puppy dog, and even though I would give him yet another stern talking to about drinking, now was not the time for that.

"So, you hid on my ship, hiding in plain sight as I went on a wild goose chase, now what? Why are you on my ship?" I asked.

"Every trial needs a jury," Naples said. "And what better jury than Harry Tucker's friends?"

"You can't do this...!" Harry yelled from his broken position on the deck. He rose up on his arms, beaten and gaunt – slobbers came from the crook of his mouth. "These people should not be brought into this... this doesn't concern them. This is between you and me, no one else."

"You're wrong," Naples said in an acidy tone. "If I can prove to your friends the crimes in which you are guilty of, then those who you harmed will be able to rest easy when you face your punishment."

For the first time I looked at Harry in a different light. Gone was the burly, hard-pressed man, replaced by a man haggard and deposed. *Those who you harmed,* meant that Harry killed, or had a hand in killing people. *Perhaps it was war,* I told myself, but my gut told me that was unlikely.

24

"Get to the wheelhouse," Naples told the Arab. "Set our course for the island. We have a long overdue wrong to right."

After liberating my stateroom of firearms, Naples locked us inside, leaving the Texan on guard outside the door. The sound of the *Algiers'* engines came alive seconds later, and Crocker mumbled something about pistons, and hoped the pirates didn't burn up his engines.

"There are only four of them, and one of them is a woman," Lucas said. "Why didn't we take them?"

"Because they have guns," I replied and added, "And don't underestimate a woman. They are stronger than you might think, especially when they are on a vendetta." I turned toward Harry. He lied on my couch as the Major tended to his wounds.

"It's amazing you're even conscious, considering the trauma you took to your head," Ronald said as he applied a cold compress to Harry's forehead.

"What's going on, Harry?" I asked. "Does Naples have a claim to what she said out there?"

Harry only stared at me. His eyes were milky white and lifeless, as if the spark had gone out of him. I've seen men broken before and in all the other instances, that which broke them was real, and damning.

"Harry, we can't help you if you won't talk to us," I said.

"Just leave me alone," Harry managed to mumble. He turned his face away from me and let out a painful sigh.

"Damn it, Harry!" I grumbled. "Is any of what Naples said true?"

Ronald stood away from Harry and laid a hand on my shoulder. "Shouting at him won't get any answers," he said.

"I need to know if he is guilty," I said.

"Lad, we are all guilty of something. You of all people should know that," Ronald said with a sorrowful gaze.

I stared at Ronald, as if he just slapped me across the face. Sometimes a shock to reality is what a man needs to put things into perspective. I know my guilt is real. I live with it every day of my life, and no matter how long I live, it will always be with me.

"So, what do we do?" Crocker asked.

"I say we fight." I couldn't fault Lucas for his bravado, but with youth comes naivety.

"That's foolish," Ronald said.

"Why," Crocker asked. "I mean, the kid is right. Any other time we would be planning something. Why aren't we now?"

"Are you sober enough to even know what's going on?" I asked glaring at, Crocker.

"That's low, Zane, really low," Crocker said in a shameful tone.

I offered him an ireful glare and held my disappointment for the time being and instead, said, "We don't know the whole story of what's happening. Harry is not forthcoming, and I daresay until he is, we won't know what's happening until we get to our destination."

As night settled across the sea, and lanterns lit, the stateroom door opened to find the Texan standing in its opening. "She wants to see you," he said.

"What if I don't want to see her," I asked.

The Texan didn't reply. He just stood there waiting.

"Go with him," Ronald said. "You might find out a bit of what's going on."

Even though Ronald was right, the last thing I wanted was to be ordered around on my own ship. "Keep trying to get Harry to talk," I said heading toward the door. "If I don't come back…"

"You better come back," Lucas said. "Or we will tear this place apart."

The Texan snorted, and said with a hard tone, "Come on."

Stepping out on to the deck, the Texan gestured with his hand. "I know the way," I said. The deck was lit by a dozen lanterns posted throughout the ship. I always liked the calming haze they provided, but in this instant, I wish there was a lot more light.

"You're full of yourself, aren't you?" the Texan asked.

"In my life you have to be," I replied. "How much is she paying you strongarm types?"

"What makes you think she is?" the Texan asked.

"Hired guns usually don't work for free," I said as I navigated up the stairs toward the wheelhouse. "Mercenaries are of abundance in Southeast Asia, if you're not one I would be surprised."

"You think you have this all figured out, don't you?"

"I may not look like it," I said. "But I've lived out here long enough, and I catch on pretty easily. You have to if you're going to survive out here." I stopped on the stairs and looked back at the large man. "I've got you figured out."

"Then you know, I'll do what I must to earn my pay," the Texan said bluntly.

"And you know I'm not the kind of guy to be pushed around. I'll go along with this only so far. When I think there isn't anything more to learn, well then you know what will happen."

The Texan eyed me, and said, 'Then we have an accord."

"We do," I replied before I continued up the stairs to the wheelhouse.

I found the Arab and Naples in the dimly lit control room when I entered. The ship was moving along about eight knots, which told me none of them knew too much about sailing a steamer in the dead of night. The ocean was calm, which was a rarity, and a seasoned sailor would have kept the engine at full steam to take advantage of the stillness.

"I wanted to let you know we will be arriving at daylight," Naples said when I stepped up next to her. The Texan remained close, and I would be a fool to try anything with his forty-five pointed in my direction.

"Just where is here?" I asked.

"Vincent Sound," Naples replied. "On the island of Queensport."

"Never heard of it."

"Few have," Naples said. "Vincent Sound is... *was* an Australian colony, established in 1901 soon after Australia formed its own independence. It was a fishing colony and its population worked primarily in that industry. A small village was built, and the island thrived in its short existence."

"What's the island have to do with all of this?" I asked.

"I was born there," Naples said. "My parents were fishermen. My mother worked in a processing plant, and my *father* captained a fishing trawler."

"You said *was*. I take it Vincent Sound isn't there anymore?"

"In 1919, when I was nine, a plague broke out. It started as a simple sickness but spread quickly. In the first week twenty-two people died, and it was feared that everyone would succumb to its potency."

"But they didn't, did they?" I asked.

"No," Naples said in a heavy tone. "Help was asked for, but the new Australian government was unable or unwilling to help. Starvation ran rampant and even though the plague was contained, many of the fishermen were unable to work. As a way to combat the famine, rations were sanctioned, but when it was discovered that even that wouldn't be possible, the island minister created a secret lottery, those chosen were put to death by poison, presumably so others could live. *My* mother was one of the victims. The island minister, was Harry Tucker."

Stunned, I thought about that for a long moment. Harry never struck me as a mass murderer. A little self-centered, and a bit obstinate but basically an alright guy. I just couldn't accept that he was being painted in such a light. While it's true that Harry wouldn't help the needy or give someone a place to sleep if they didn't have any money, he wouldn't be callous for callous sake.

"You don't believe me, do you?" Naples asked.

"I'm keeping an open mind," I replied. But, no I didn't believe her, or at the very least believe what she thought she knew. She was a child when her story happened. Her memories might have been marred with time and anger, that could have altered her perception. While I didn't doubt that the plague happened, I did doubt her recollection.

"You said your mother succumbed to the poison," I said. "But what happened to your father?"

Naples was quiet and she stared out at the black sea in front of us. Her breathing was shallow, and she fought to keep control of her emotions. When she drew a breath to speak, I heard the grief in her breath, then the anger in her words when she said, "Harry Tucker *is* my father."

I drew a breath to speak, but Naples didn't give me a chance and she told the Texan, "Take him back below, and bring the others out onto deck. It will be daylight soon."

"Did you know Harry," I asked him when he appeared out of the stateroom. "Did you know she was your daughter?"

Harry's eyes were heavy and when he looked at me, I saw the remorse in them. "Not at first," he admitted. "Not during the poker game. I had too much to drink, the saloon was crazy, and I was too concerned with winning some money. You know how it is."

"Yeah, I know how it is," I replied.

Under gunpoint, the Texan and Arab herded us all out onto deck. The new day haze along the surface of the water was so thick it almost looked like a concrete sidewalk. The

Algiers was anchored off the shore of the island.. In the distance there was a marina, but the fog consumed it and its details alluded me.

Harry recovered some, but he still needed assistance, and Crocker helped him, allowing Harry to use him as a crutch.

"What's this all about, Zane?" Ronald whispered.

How could I sum up in a few seconds what I learned. I just gave the Major a look, and hoped he understood my silence.

"How long has it been, father?" Naples asked when she came up behind us. All eyes went to her. "Do you remember the smell of death; do you remember the cries in the night? I do."

Harry didn't say anything, he didn't even look at Naples, and instead he stared at the floor like a man guilty of the crimes he had been accused. When he spoke, his words were burdensome. "No matter what I say in my defense, you've already convicted me. There is nothing I can say to prove my innocence."

"That's because there is none," Naples said in a calm maniacal tone.

"What do you hope to prove here," I asked. "If you have already convicted your father, anything you do from this point forward, is for your own self-righteousness."

Naples' smile was callous, and she replied in an even tone, "I believed I've earned it. I've spent my whole life to get to this point. I will not squander it by allowing Harry an easy death."

"I don't really know what's going on here, child," Ronald said. "But feeding hate with hate is never a good thing. If Harry is guilty of something, he should be given a fair trial, not be subject to a kangaroo court such as this."

Regarding Ronald, Naples' expression lightened some and she said, "All will be revealed in due time." When her gaze went back to Harry, her words were forceful and direct, "Get the rowboat launched and get them aboard."

Harry didn't look at anyone as we made the crossing. Lucas and Crocker were made to row the boat to the island under gunpoint as the Texan and Arab faced them from the bow, as Naples sat at the stern next to the third hired man in her employ. Ronald and I sat with our backs to them and as we approach the pier, I filled him in on everything I learned regarding Naples and Harry. Ronald listened intently understanding what was going to happen once we reached the village of Vincent Sound.

As the rowboat approached the remnants of the once thriving settlement, it was apparent that no one had been to the island in a very long time.

Without maintenance, some of the marina had sunk below the surface. There were three fishing boats moored to the pylons and they were caked with dark green algae and had become bird sanctuaries for the local fowl.

Once on shore, we were escorted into the town. The surrounding forest had begun to reclaim the settlement. There wasn't a building in the square that hadn't been touched by some type of overgrowth.

"There," Naples said pointing at a series of chairs in the center of the square. They faced a makeshift podium, and it was evident that Naples and her crew had been here before, to set things up. "We will hold the trial there," she said.

Shoved toward the seats, my crew and I were made to sit behind the accused. Behind us sat the Texan and the Arab. Naples stood at the podium, wrapping a gavel on top of the stand, and with authority, said, "The citizens of Vincent Sound verses Harry Tucker for the crime of mass murder. How does the accused plead?"

Before Harry could open his mouth, Naples said, "Let it be read into the record that the accused pleads guilty."

Ronald went to his feet and said with weight to his words, "See here. If this man is to stand trial, he should be represented in some way."

Naples' lips formed a hard little line, and she said, "Are you offering your services as lawyer pro-temp for the accused?"

Ronald looked down at me, and I shook my head no, even though I knew what he was going to say. "I do," he announced. *Damn it,* I grumbled to myself.

Iniquitous, Naples said, "Let it be known then, Major that you will share the accused's fate with him."

Shooting to my feet, I sensed movement behind me, as the Arab and Texan stood, standing ready in case I got too rambunctious. With authority in my tone I yelled, "He will *not*. No member of my crew will be held accountable for something they had no part of."

"You are all accused," Naples said.

"But why?" I demanded.

Naples leaned on the podium, as she said, "You went to great lengths to find and protect your friend. If I hadn't commandeered your vessel, you would have tracked down my yacht in an attempt to stop me from seeking justice."

"Your reasoning has no logic," Ronald said. "You must show concrete evidence that Harry Tucker is indeed guilty of the crimes you accuse him of. Otherwise, you are guilty yourself."

"This isn't a trial," I proclaimed. "Harry is being disposed of. You aren't seeking justice but revenge. Your mind is clouded by memories of a nine-year-old."

"Enough of this," Naples said repeatedly slamming the gavel on top of the podium. "Seize him." she jabbed a finger in my direction.

When the third member of her mercenaries came forward, Crocker leapt from his seated position on top of the man, clobbering him across the face with a couple heavy handed punches. The Texan turned toward Crocker leveling his pistol on my engineer, but Ronald jumped in between them as the Texan fired his pistol. The slug slammed into the Major's shoulder sending him to the ground.

"Ronald...!" I exclaimed but was held back by the Arab. I swung my body toward Naples and shouted, "You say you're seeking justice, but all you do is create chaos...! How long will it be before you kill someone, in an effort to bring a man to justice for murders you can't prove?"

"I've had all I'm going to take from you! Lash him to the pole!" Naples ordered.

34

I don't know why I didn't see it before, but several yards from the podium stood a tall wooden pole and stacked around it several cords of firewood. This wasn't proving to be a good day for me. I spent my life one step ahead of the law, one day away from being captured by bounty hunters, only to find myself burned to death. *Hell no...!*

I slugged the Arab, who reached out for me as I bolted. Snagging me by the shirt, it ripped, and I only managed to slip out of his clutches to fall into the hands of the Texan who shoved his pistol in my gut. "You know, sooner or later I'm going to take that gun from you and shove it down your throat," I snarled as he shoved me toward the pole.

Tied to the pole, my crew stood in shock as the tall Texan came forward with a burning torch. I gulped. This was happening, this was actually happening. I leaned my head against the splintery wood behind me. I'm not an overly religious man, I believe in God, but rarely did I ever pray to him. This was an occasion that needed to be prayed for. If the big guy in the sky was going to do anything, it needed to happen now.

Harry Tucker went to his feet, and shouted, "You can't do this... you can't kill my friend!"

Naples ignored him, and waved a hand at the Texan who threw the torch into the wood. In an instant the woodpile roared to life.

"Zane was right," Harry said. "Your memories are clouded. You were only a child with no understanding of what was truly going on. I did everything I could to save the people of this village and I knew then, there was nothing I could do but watch them die from starvation. But it wasn't

I who orchestrated the horrible events that took place after the plague. I tried to stop her, I tried to tell her it wasn't an option. But your mother wouldn't listen to me, and she took matters into her own hands. It wasn't I who poisoned the citizens of Vincent Sound; it was your mother."

"*Liar*," Naples shouted.

"I am guilty," Harry confessed as the flames shot over my head. "I am guilty of the death of your mother at my hands, I am guilty of not being the father you needed, and I am guilty of abandoning you, unable to face you for my sin."

By the expression on Naples' face, she knew the revelation to be true and as she dropped to her knees expelling an agonizing scream, the blistering heat consumed me.

When the Texan went to Naples' side, Crocker and Lucas sprang into action, both of them tackling the remaining mercenaries, Crocker on top of the Arab and Lucas pinning the third man to the ground. Hacking and coughing from the intense smoke, I knew this was the end.

Suddenly, a form leapt through the high flames and Harry came to my side. "Hold on Zane... hold on I got you," he said.

When the ropes went loose at my side, Harry took me in his arms, but he let go of me when Naples came into the inferno. She clawed at Harry's face, shouting, "You killed her, you killed her, you killed her!"

Your mother was crazed, incensed, and out of her mind," Harry exclaimed. "If I hadn't stopped her, it's hard to tell how many more people she would've murdered before help arrived."

"Murderer!" Naples dug deeper in her attack and Harry instinctively slapped her away. She lost her footing and fell into the ever-growing fire; her screams were ones of failure and realization, as she succumbed to the flames.

I grabbed Harry and threw him out of the fire as I jumped behind him landing at the feet of the Texan. Weak and my energy spent I drew in some hidden strength as I went to my feet taking him by surprise and clobbering the large man to the ground. Through smoke filled eyes I glanced to find the Texan's .45 at my feet and scooped it up shoving the end of it, into his face. "You move and you're dead," I hacked out.

Ronald came to my side holding a handkerchief at his bleeding shoulder. "It's over Zane," he said.

I glanced over to Harry who stood at the burning pyre, and I said, "Yes, it is, but it will be a long time for the healing to staunch what happened here today."

The *Algiers* cut a swath through the ocean on its way home. I left Lucas in the wheelhouse and joined Harry at the stern of the ship. The day was ending as the sun sank on the horizon. "Our prisoners are locked in the hold, and the Major is resting," I said leaning on the railing. The salty air stung my tender flesh and I felt like a roasted Thanksgiving turkey. "We will be home in a day or two. Are you going to be alright?"

"I swore a secret promise that I would protect her, that I would spare her the truth," Harry said not taking his eyes from the churning water behind the ship.

Painfully honest, I said, "There was no saving Naples, she had made up her mind long before today."

"Her name was Emery," Harry said in a somber tone. "That woman who died back there, that wasn't my little girl." He gripped the railing and wept.

Unable to find the right words, I simply reached up and placed a hand on Harry's shoulder.

FIN-

ABOUT THE AUTHOR

Charles F. Millhouse is an Award-Winning Author and Publisher. He published his first book in 1999 and he hasn't looked back. He has written over forty published works including novels and short stories. From the 1930's adventures of Captain Hawklin – through the gritty paranormal old west town of New Kingdom – to the far-off future in the Origin Trilogy. Charles' imagination is boundless. He breathes life into his characters, brings worlds alive and sends his readers on journeys they won't soon forget.

Charles lives in Southeastern, Ohio with his wife and two sons.

Visit stormgatepress.com for more details.